To Mum and Dad. Thank you.
K.M.

A TEMPLAR BOOK

First published in the UK in 2016 by Templar Publishing,
part of the Bonnier Publishing Group,
The Plaza, 535 King's Road, London, SW10 0SZ
www.templarco.co.uk
www.bonnierpublishing.com

1 3 5 7 9 10 8 6 4 2

ISBN 978-1-78370-591-7 Hardback
ISBN 978-1-78370-590-0 Paperback

This book was typeset in Futura
The illustrations were created with mixed media

Designed by Genevieve Webster
Edited by Katie Haworth

Printed in Poland

I am a very Clever Cat

Kasia Matyjaszek

templar publishing

Hello! My name is Stockton.
I am a **very** clever cat.

Look what I can **do** . . .

I am just **SO** smart.

But what I do best is . . .

. . . knitting!

Knitting is nothing for a **talented** cat like me.

Watch me knit the fanciest scarf for the fanciest soirée.

Bright pink will be **perfect**.

And casting on . . .

. . . is **easy!**

Who needs a pattern?

I make it up as I go along.

A stitch here . . .

. . . a loop there . . .

. . . and a **big** knot
or two.

This is going to be the **best scarf ever!**

And now for the finishing touches . . .

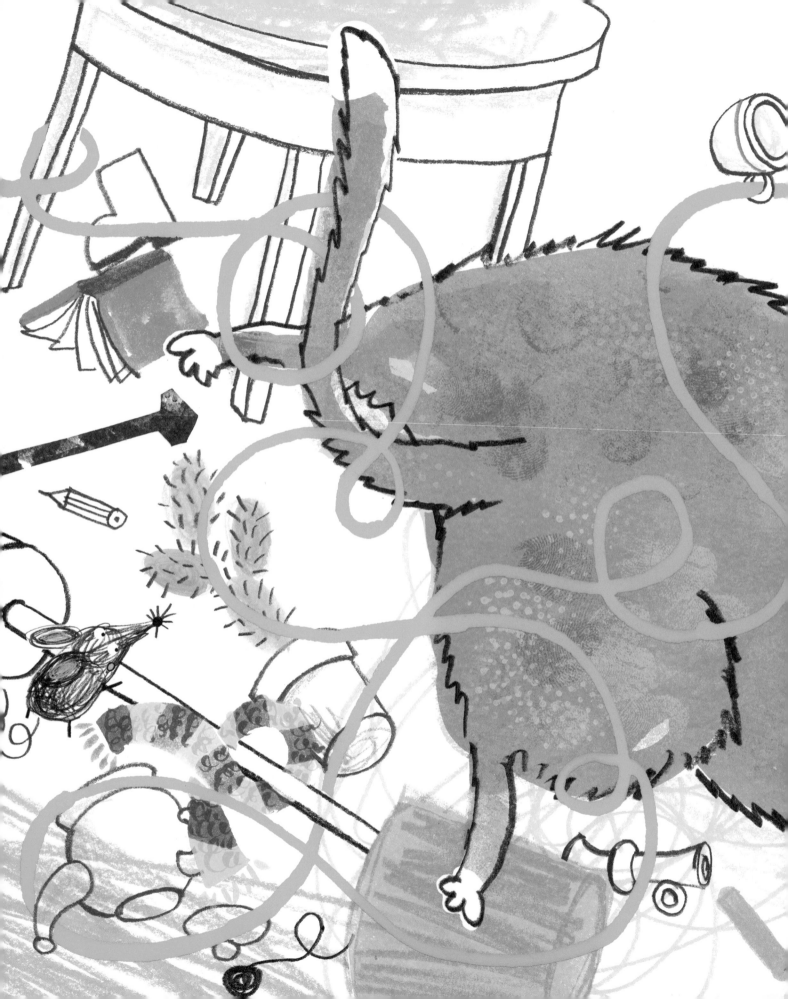

OOPS!

Oh dear. Look what I've done.

Now I'll **never** go to the fancy soirée.

But wait, what's this . . . ?

My name is Stockton
and I am a very **smart** cat . . .

. . . with some very **clever** friends.